SEGUN DOMINIC

Infinite Love Note

Contents

One

The Scarlet Thread

The aroma of freshly brewed coffee mingled with cinnamon danced through the air, a familiar comfort that greeted Nadia every morning. Sunlight slanted through the window, painting golden stripes across the worn armchair where David usually sat, a newspaper rustled beside him. But this morning, the chair was empty.

A prickle of unease snaked down Nadia's spine. David was a creature of habit, and their mornings always began with a shared cup of coffee and stolen kisses between sips of the steaming brew. She called out his name, her voice echoing in the silence of their small apartment.

Ignoring the growing worry, Nadia padded towards the kitchen, the wooden floorboards creaking beneath her bare feet. A solitary mug sat on the counter, untouched, a single red rose lying beside it, its velvety bloom a stark contrast against the stark white porcelain.

Nadia's heart skipped a beat. Red roses were their thing, a silent promise whispered between them since their first date years ago. But this one felt different, unsettling even. There was no accompanying note, no sweet message scrawled in David's familiar hand.

A sliver of apprehension gnawed at her. David wasn't one for grand gestures, but a silent rose felt…off-kilter. She brushed her fingers against the soft petals, a shiver tracing down her spine as a tiny, rolled-up piece of parchment tumbled from the heart of the rose.

Unfurling the paper with trembling fingers, Nadia's breath hitched. The stark white surface held a single line, written in a spidery script that sent a jolt of ice through her veins.

"Always remember, even love can wear a mask."

The world seemed to tilt on its axis. The playful banter, the stolen glances, the whispered promises under starlit skies – could it all have been a lie? A cold dread seeped into her bones, replacing the warmth of the morning sun.

Nadia reread the note, the simple sentence morphing into a monstrous question mark that loomed over their entire relationship. Doubt, a seed she'd never allowed to take root, began to sprout, its tendrils coiling around her heart.

Memories flickered through her mind like frames from a forgotten film. David's occasional late nights at the office, the hushed phone calls he always took outside, the guarded silences that had become more frequent in recent months.

Had she been so blinded by love that she'd ignored the subtle cracks in the facade? Or was this some elaborate prank, a misguided attempt to rekindle the spark in their relationship?

She stormed into the bedroom, her eyes scanning the room for any other clues. On the bedside table, nestled amongst the clutter of books and papers, lay a worn leather-bound journal. It wasn't David's – the rich brown cover bore the inscription "E.A." in elegant lettering.

Hesitantly, Nadia picked it up. The worn leather felt cool and smooth in her hands. A sliver of guilt pricked her conscience as she contemplated opening it, but the cryptic note gnawed at her, urging her to uncover the truth.

With a deep breath, she cracked open the journal, the musty scent of aged paper filling her senses. The first page was filled with flowing prose, a love letter that poured out its heart in words both passionate and tender.

A pang of familiarity shot through Nadia. The turn of phrase, the raw vulnerability – it echoed a voice she knew all too well, David's voice. But the signature at the bottom shattered the illusion: E.A.

The air hung heavy in the silent room. The weight of the unknown pressed down on Nadia, suffocating her. In her hand, the love letter transformed into a weapon, each word a fresh blow.

Just then, the shrill ring of her phone pierced the silence. It was David, his voice laced with concern as he apologized for the missing breakfast and promised to be home soon. Nadia forced a smile, her voice tight as she mumbled a reply.

As she hung up, the red rose on the counter seemed to mock her. Love, she thought, a bitter taste rising in her throat. How easily it could be twisted, how quickly a promise could turn into a lie.

The day stretched before her, an empty canvas waiting to be filled. But the colors at her disposal were no longer vibrant hues of love and trust. Today, the palette held only shades of doubt, suspicion, and a chilling fear of the truth that lay hidden beneath the surface.

Two

Echoes in the Fog

The day crawled by for Nadia, each tick of the clock echoing the relentless drumbeat of her unease. David's apologetic texts offered little solace. The cryptic note and the mysterious journal gnawed at her, urging her to take action.

By evening, the apartment felt suffocating. Nadia grabbed her bag and a worn denim jacket, the familiar weight offering a sliver of comfort. She needed answers, and with a growing sense of trepidation, she decided to start with the inscription on the journal – E.A.

A quick internet search yielded limited results. E.A. could be anyone, from a forgotten childhood friend to a literary pseudonym. But one name stood out – a local art gallery co-owned by a pair of siblings, Ethan and Amelia Rose.

A sliver of hope, fragile as a spiderweb, fluttered in Nadia's chest. Could this be a coincidence? Or was it a connection, a thread in the unraveling tapestry of her life?

The art gallery occupied a quaint two-story building in the heart of Ado Ekiti. Stepping inside, Nadia was greeted by a cool hush and the scent of oil paints and old books. An eclectic mix of paintings and sculptures adorned the walls, casting an otherworldly glow under the soft lighting.

Behind the counter stood a young woman, her fiery red hair pulled back in a messy bun. Her eyes, the color of deep emeralds, widened in surprise as Nadia approached.

"Excuse me," Nadia began, her voice barely a whisper. "I was wondering if you might know someone by the initials E.A.?"

The woman's smile faltered for a brief moment, a flicker of something Nadia couldn't decipher passing through her eyes. "Actually, that would be us," she replied, gesturing towards herself. "Ethan and Amelia Rose."

Relief washed over Nadia, momentarily erasing the knot of tension in her stomach. "Oh, thank goodness," she sighed. "I found a journal with those initials and I thought..."

Her voice trailed off as a man emerged from behind a large canvas, a paintbrush clutched in his hand. He was tall and lean, with a mop of unruly brown hair and eyes that held a hint of amusement.

"Amelia," he said, his voice a warm baritone, "who's our visitor?"

"This is Nadia," Amelia replied, her gaze fixed on Nadia. "She was looking for someone by the initials E.A."

The man's smile faltered slightly. He studied Nadia for a long moment, his eyes filled with a question she couldn't answer.

"Perhaps we should step into my office," he said finally, gesturing towards a doorway hidden behind a tapestry.

Nadia hesitated, her heart pounding against her ribs. A part of her craved answers, but another part recoiled from the unknown. Yet, the truth beckoned, a siren song she couldn't resist.

Taking a deep breath, Nadia followed the man, her footsteps echoing on the polished wooden floor. The office was a stark contrast to the gallery – small, cluttered, and filled with the personal effects that spoke of a life well-lived.

"Please, sit," the man said, gesturing towards a worn leather armchair. He introduced himself as Ethan, Amelia's brother.

Nadia explained how she'd found the journal, her voice trembling slightly. As she spoke, she noticed a flicker of recognition in Ethan's eyes, a fleeting emotion she couldn't quite place.

"The journal," Ethan said finally, his voice thoughtful. "It belonged to Amelia.

But it… it shouldn't be out there."

A cold dread coiled around Nadia's heart. "Why not?" she managed to ask, her voice barely a whisper.

Ethan and Amelia exchanged a glance, a silent conversation passing between them. The air in the room crackled with unspoken tension.

"Nadia," Amelia said finally, her voice laced with a hint of sympathy, "the things written in that journal… they're part of the past. A past that's best left undisturbed."

But for Nadia, the past was no longer a distant land. It had bled into her present, staining the vibrant tapestry of her love story with doubt. And she wouldn't rest until she unraveled the truth, no matter how unsettling it might be.

Three

Whispers in the Dark

Nadia left the art gallery with a head full of questions and a heart heavy with a growing sense of betrayal. Ethan and Amelia's veiled warnings only intensified her determination to unearth the truth buried within the pages of the journal.

Back in the solitude of her apartment, Nadia reread the entries, each word a shard of a shattered mirror reflecting a distorted reality. The love letters, penned with such passion and tenderness, were addressed to someone named "Aisha," not Nadia.

Aisha. The name echoed in the stillness of the room, a stranger intruding upon the sacred space of Nadia's relationship. She scoured the internet, searching for any trace of this Aisha, this woman who had seemingly possessed David's heart before Nadia.

The search yielded nothing but frustration. Yet, a nagging suspicion wouldn't let go. The journal entries spoke of stolen moments, clandestine meetings, a love that thrived in the shadows. It was a stark contrast to the openness and honesty that had been the cornerstone of Nadia and David's relationship.

Night fell, cloaking the city in an inky blackness. Sleep evaded Nadia. Every rustle of leaves outside her window, every creak of the floorboards sent a jolt of fear through her. The once familiar comfort of her apartment now felt alien, tainted by the shadows of doubt.

The following morning, Nadia decided to confront David. The thought of it twisted her insides into a knot of apprehension, but the need for answers outweighed her fear.

David arrived home from work looking weary. His smile faltered slightly as he saw the grim expression on Nadia's face. Before he could speak, she thrust the journal at him, her voice trembling with a mix of anger and hurt.

"What is this?" she demanded, her voice barely a whisper.

David's face drained of color as he stared at the worn leather cover. He hesitated for a long moment, then snatched the journal from her grasp.

"Where did you get this?" he asked, his voice tight with barely concealed anger.

"That doesn't matter," Nadia retorted, her voice gaining strength. "What matters is who Aisha is, and why you were writing love letters to her!"

David's jaw clenched, his eyes hardening with a flicker of something Nadia couldn't decipher. The playful, loving man she knew seemed to vanish, replaced by a stranger shrouded in secrets.

"Nadia," he began, his voice low and strained, "there's an explanation for this, but—"

His words were cut short by a loud banging on the front door. Nadia's heart leaped into her throat. David exchanged a panicked look with her, then hurried towards the door.

He opened it a crack, his voice guarded as he spoke to someone on the other side. Nadia strained to hear, but the conversation was muffled. Finally, David closed the door, his face pale and drawn.

"Who was it?" Nadia demanded, her unease growing with every passing second.

David hesitated, then sighed deeply. "It was nothing," he muttered, his eyes avoiding hers.

But the lie was evident in the tremor of his voice and the nervous twitch of his jaw. Nadia knew better than to believe him. The journal, the cryptic note, the unexpected visitor – they were all pieces of a puzzle that didn't quite fit.

And Nadia was determined to find the missing piece, even if it meant uncovering a truth that could shatter the foundation of her world.

Four

A Trail of Breadcrumbs

The unwelcome visitor cast a long shadow over Nadia's already troubled mind. David's unconvincing explanation and the tremor in his voice fueled her suspicion. Sleep was a distant memory, replaced by a relentless replay of the day's events and a fervent hope of piecing together the puzzle of her fractured reality.

The journal remained on the table, an unwelcome guest spewing secrets Nadia wasn't sure she was prepared to face. Yet, its worn pages held a morbid allure, a promise of answers that both terrified and compelled her.

With a deep breath, Nadia flipped through the entries, searching for any clues about Aisha's identity or her connection to David. A particular passage grabbed her attention. It spoke of a hidden place, a sanctuary where their love could blossom away from prying eyes – "The Whispering Palms," it was called.

The name sent a jolt through Nadia. The Whispering Palms was a secluded grove on the outskirts of Ado Ekiti, a place shrouded in local folklore and whispered legends. It was said to be a place of both beauty and danger, a haven for outcasts and those seeking refuge from the outside world.

Could this be the place where David met Aisha? A sliver of hope, fragile as a spiderweb, fluttered in Nadia's chest. Perhaps this was the key to unlocking the secrets of the past, the missing piece in the puzzle of David's deception.

The following morning, Nadia rose with a newfound determination. David was gone, a note left on the kitchen counter stating he had a prior work commitment. Nadia couldn't ignore the pang of suspicion that accompanied his absence.

She decided to act. Dressing in comfortable clothes and grabbing a worn backpack, she hailed a taxi and headed towards the outskirts of town. The drive was long and arduous, the dusty road snaking through a landscape of sparse vegetation and towering termite mounds.

Finally, the taxi driver pointed towards a cluster of palm trees swaying gently in the distance. "The Whispering Palms," he muttered, his voice laced with a hint of apprehension.

Nadia paid the fare and stepped out, the heat pressing down on her like a heavy cloak. The air hung thick with an unsettling silence, broken only by the rustle of leaves in the dry wind. As she ventured deeper into the grove, an unsettling feeling prickled at her skin. The towering palms cast long, grotesque shadows on the dusty ground, and the silence was so profound it felt like a living entity.

Suddenly, a twig snapped behind her. Nadia whirled around, her heart pounding in her chest. But there was nothing there, only the unsettling rustle of leaves and the ever-present silence.

She pressed on, her senses on high alert. The air grew cooler, the dense foliage overhead filtering out the harsh sunlight. The path narrowed, transforming into a labyrinth of twisted roots and fallen leaves.

Then, she saw it. A clearing bathed in an ethereal glow, sunlight filtering through the leaves to paint dappled patterns on the soft grass. In the center stood a small, weathered cabin, its paint peeling and windows boarded shut.

An unfamiliar sense of dread washed over Nadia. This place, shrouded in mystery and whispered secrets, felt charged with a hidden energy. With a deep breath, she approached the cabin, her hand instinctively reaching for the pepper spray tucked away in her backpack.

Reaching the doorway, she hesitated. The silence pressed in on her, thick and suffocating. But the need for answers propelled her forward. Taking a deep breath, she pushed open the creaky door.

The interior of the cabin was dark and dusty, the air heavy with the scent of neglect and damp earth. Moonlight streamed through a broken window, illuminating cobweb-draped furniture and a lone, overturned chair.

As Nadia's eyes adjusted to the dim light, a glint of metal caught her attention. In the corner, half-buried beneath a pile of fallen leaves, lay a glinting object. Nadia knelt down, her heart hammering against her ribs, and brushed away the debris.

It was a locket, a silver heart engraved with a single entwined letter – A. Nadia's breath hitched. The locket felt cold in her hand, a tangible link to the woman who had haunted her for days.

With a trembling hand, she pried it open. Nestled inside was a faded photograph, the edges worn and frayed. The picture depicted a young woman, her smile radiant, her eyes filled with a warmth that mirrored the love expressed in David's journal entries.

But it wasn't just any woman. It was Aisha.

Five

The Weight of a Past

The faded photograph in the locket felt heavy in Nadia's hand, a physical manifestation of a truth she could barely comprehend. Staring into Aisha's warm eyes, Nadia felt a strange mix of emotions – anger, betrayal, and a flicker of something akin to empathy.

Who was Aisha? What was the nature of her relationship with David? And what dark secrets lay hidden within the walls of this abandoned cabin?

Questions swirled in Nadia's mind, a relentless storm threatening to consume her. But amidst the chaos, a single thought surfaced, sharp and clear – she needed to find David.

Leaving the cabin behind, Nadia emerged into the clearing. The once serene grove now felt menacing, the shadows of the palm trees dancing like phantoms in the fading light. As she retraced her steps, a twig snapped behind her, sending a jolt of fear through her.

Spinning around, she scanned the dense foliage, her heart hammering against her ribs. But there was nothing, only the unsettling silence of the grove mocking her apprehension.

Pushing onward, Nadia quickened her pace. The walk back seemed longer, the path more treacherous. Every rustle of leaves, every creak of a branch sent a fresh wave of panic washing over her.

Finally, she emerged from the grove, blinking in the golden light of the setting sun. Relief flooded her momentarily, but it was quickly replaced by a new surge of worry. How would she confront David? What would she say?

Reaching the main road, Nadia flagged down a passing taxi and narrated her experience at the Whispering Palms, omitting the part about the locket. The driver listened intently, his eyes widening at the mention of the secluded grove.

"That place," he muttered, his voice laced with a hint of fear, "it's not for the curious. Many have gone in seeking answers, but few have returned unchanged."

Nadia's unease deepened. The Whispering Palms seemed to hold more secrets than she could have ever imagined. Back in her apartment, the silence felt suffocating. David still hadn't returned, and his unanswered calls only amplified her growing anxiety.

As night fell, Nadia decided to take action. She grabbed her laptop and opened David's work email, an act she'd never dared to do before. Driven by a desperate need for answers, she typed in his password, a combination they'd always shared – their anniversary.

To her surprise, the login was successful. Shame washed over her as she scrolled through his inbox, but the urgency of the situation eclipsed her guilt. A particular email caught her eye – addressed to an anonymous recipient with the subject line "The Grove."

Her heart pounded as she clicked it open. The email was brief, containing only a single sentence: "Meet me at the cabin tomorrow night. Come alone."

A cold dread coiled around Nadia's heart. David was planning to meet someone at the Whispering Palms, the place shrouded in mystery and danger. The recipient – was it Aisha?

Suddenly, the pieces of the puzzle began to fall into place. The cryptic note, the hidden journal, David's secretive behavior – it all pointed towards a past he desperately wanted to keep buried.

But Nadia wouldn't let him. Not anymore. Armed with the email and the locket, she knew what she had to do. The truth, however unsettling it might be, was the only path forward.

Six

Rendezvous in the Shadows

The night air hung heavy with anticipation as Nadia crept towards the clearing bathed in moonlight. The Whispering Palms, once a source of unsettling curiosity, now beckoned with a dark allure. David's email, a stark message promising a clandestine meeting at the abandoned cabin, echoed in her mind.

Fear prickled at Nadia's skin, but it was overshadowed by a fierce determination to confront the truth. Clad in dark clothing and armed with a flashlight and a pepper spray, she navigated the treacherous path, her senses on high alert.

Reaching the clearing, Nadia crouched behind a gnarled tree trunk, its shadow offering a fragile cloak of concealment. The cabin loomed ahead, its windows dark and empty. A low growl rumbled in her stomach – the last thing she'd eaten was a hastily grabbed sandwich hours ago.

Suddenly, a flicker of movement caught her eye. A figure emerged from the shadows, their form obscured by the darkness. Her heart hammered against her ribs as she gripped the pepper spray tighter in her hand.

"David?" she called out, her voice barely a whisper.

The figure hesitated, then stepped into the moonlight. Relief washed over Nadia, momentarily erasing the knot of tension in her stomach. It was David, his face etched with worry as his eyes scanned the clearing.

"Nadia? What are you doing here?" he demanded, his voice laced with a mixture of surprise and anger.

Before Nadia could respond, a new voice cut through the tense silence. "David?"

A woman stepped out from behind the cabin, her voice soft yet filled with a tremor of emotion. The moonlight illuminated her features – Aisha.

Nadia's breath hitched. Aisha was older than in the photograph, but the warmth in her eyes remained undimmed. A storm of emotions – anger, betrayal, and a strange sense of empathy – warred within Nadia.

"Aisha," David breathed, his voice thick with a mix of relief and apprehension. "I... I didn't expect to see you here."

The reunion, if one could call it that, was charged with unspoken words and a palpable tension. Nadia watched, a silent observer in this unfolding drama.

"I got your message," Aisha said, her gaze fixed on David. "I had to come."

"There must be some misunderstanding," David stammered, his eyes darting nervously between Nadia and Aisha. "There's no message—"

"Don't lie, David," Aisha interrupted, her voice hardening. "We both know why I'm here."

A strained silence descended upon the clearing, broken only by the chirping of crickets and the rustle of leaves in the night breeze. Nadia felt like a voyeur, witnessing a secret chapter of David's life laid bare under the cold scrutiny of the moon.

Finally, Nadia stepped out from behind the tree, her voice laced with a steely resolve. "There is no misunderstanding, David," she said. "I know everything."

David's head snapped towards her, his face a mask of shock and betrayal. Aisha's gaze flickered to Nadia, a flicker of recognition passing through her eyes.

"Nadia," David stammered, his voice laced with desperation. "You shouldn't be here. This doesn't concern you."

But it did concern her. Their entire relationship, built on trust and shared dreams, now lay in ruins, shattered by the secrets David had kept buried for so long.

"Tell me everything, David," Nadia demanded, her voice trembling slightly but her eyes unwavering. "Tell me about Aisha. Tell me about the lies."

David hesitated, his gaze flitting between the two women who held his past and present hostage in the moonlit clearing. The air crackled with unspoken words and the weight of a truth that threatened to consume them all.

As David opened his mouth to speak, a twig snapped in the distance. All heads turned towards the source of the sound. A solitary figure emerged from the darkness, his face obscured by the shadows.

"There you are," the figure rasped, his voice laced with menace. "Finally, the reunion is complete."

Seven

Unmasked

The menacing voice sent a jolt of fear through the clearing. Nadia, David, and Aisha whipped around, their gazes fixed on the figure emerging from the shadows. The moonlight cast an eerie glow on his tall frame, revealing a worn trench coat and a wide-brimmed hat that concealed most of his face.

"Who are you?" David demanded, his voice tight with apprehension.

The figure chuckled, a dry, humorless sound that echoed through the silent grove. "Someone who knows your secrets, David," he rasped. "Someone who has been waiting for this moment for a very long time."

Nadia's heart hammered against her ribs. The cryptic note, the abandoned cabin, the sudden appearance of Aisha – it all seemed to be connected to this shadowy figure. But what secrets did David hold, and why would someone target him in this way?

"What do you want?" Aisha stepped forward, her voice surprisingly steady despite the tremor in her hands.

The figure tilted his head, his shadowed eyes seeming to bore into her. "Justice, Aisha," he replied, his voice dripping with venom. "Justice for what you took from me."

Aisha's breath hitched. She exchanged a panicked glance with David, a silent conversation passing between them that Nadia couldn't decipher.

"I don't know what you're talking about," David stammered, his voice laced with a mixture of fear and defiance.

"Don't play dumb, David," the figure sneered. "You know exactly what I'm talking about. The accident, the stolen future – you can't escape the past forever."

The word "accident" hung heavy in the air, a dark cloud casting a shadow over the already tense situation. Nadia's mind raced, piecing together fragments of information – the love letters in the journal, the clandestine meetings, the veiled warnings from Amelia.

Suddenly, a horrible realization dawned on her. The accident – it wasn't just a random event from David's past. It was somehow connected to Aisha, and this vengeful figure seeking retribution.

"Leave him alone," Aisha pleaded, stepping closer to the figure. "This is between us. Whatever happened, it was my fault."

The figure let out a harsh laugh. "Your fault? Don't be ridiculous, Aisha. You were the victim, not the perpetrator."

His words fueled a fire of curiosity and a surge of protectiveness within Nadia. She couldn't help but feel a sliver of sympathy for Aisha, a woman caught in the crossfire of a past she desperately wanted to outrun.

"Tell us what happened," Nadia said, her voice surprisingly steady. "Tell us the truth."

The figure hesitated, then slowly lowered his hat, revealing a face etched with deep lines and haunted eyes. It was a face Nadia didn't recognize, yet it sent a shiver down her spine.

"My name is Michael," he rasped, his voice raw with emotion. "And Aisha… Aisha was supposed to be my wife."

A collective gasp escaped their lips. Michael's revelation painted a new picture, a tragic love story twisted by a cruel twist of fate. The accident – it had taken away not just a future, but a life, a love that Michael clearly cherished.

Aisha's eyes welled up with tears. "Michael, I…" she stammered, her voice choked with emotion. But before she could finish, Michael held up a hand, silencing her.

"The guilt has consumed you for years, Aisha," he said, his voice softer now, tinged with a hint of sadness. "But it wasn't your fault. It was an accident, a terrible, unforeseen tragedy."

His words seemed to hang in the air, a fragile peace offering amidst the storm of emotions. Nadia watched, torn between anger at David's deception and a newfound understanding of the forces that had shaped their lives.

The clearing was bathed in an unsettling silence, broken only by the chirping of crickets and the ragged breaths of the people caught in this web of secrets. The truth, once buried, now lay bare, casting long shadows on their present.

But even as a semblance of understanding emerged, a new question gnawed at Nadia. Why, after all these years, had Michael chosen to confront them now? And what did he intend to do next? The answer, shrouded in the darkness, sent a fresh wave of trepidation rippling through the clearing.

Eight

Shattered Pieces

The revelation hung heavy in the air, a suffocating weight pressing down on the clearing. Michael's tear-filled eyes, a stark contrast to the cold fury that had initially radiated from him, held a depth of pain that mirrored Nadia's own turmoil.

Aisha, her face streaked with tears, took a tentative step towards Michael. "I… I'm so sorry," she whispered, her voice barely audible.

Michael's gaze softened as he met her eyes. "There's nothing to apologize for," he replied, his voice gruff but laced with a hint of empathy. "It was fate's cruel hand that dealt the cards."

Nadia watched their exchange, a tangle of emotions warring within her. Anger at David's deception still simmered, but it was overshadowed by a newfound understanding of the tragic events that had shaped their lives.

David, on the other hand, remained silent, his face a mask of guilt and regret. The facade of their happy relationship, built on a foundation of hidden truths, had crumbled before his eyes.

Suddenly, a guttural growl ripped through the clearing, shattering the fragile peace that had momentarily settled. Michael flinched, his hand instinctively reaching for his pocket.

"Don't even think about it," a voice rasped from the shadows.

A new figure emerged from behind a towering palm tree, his tall frame shrouded in darkness. In his hand, a glinting firearm pointed directly at Michael.

Panic surged through Nadia. The unexpected arrival of the armed figure, his menacing presence, transformed the tense situation into a full-blown hostage crisis.

"Who are you?" David demanded, his voice trembling slightly.

"Someone who wants to ensure justice is served," the figure sneered, his voice distorted by the darkness. "Someone who won't let you walk away from your past."

David's eyes darted nervously between the armed figure and Michael. The guilt etched on his face was undeniable, a stark contrast to the carefree man Nadia had fallen in love with.

"This isn't about David anymore," Michael retorted, his voice surprisingly steady despite the gun pointed at him. "This is between me and Aisha. We need to settle this, for ourselves and for those we've lost."

Aisha stepped forward, her gaze fixed on the armed figure. "He's right," she said, her voice firm. "This is our burden to bear."

The tension in the clearing was thick enough to cut with a knife. Michael and Aisha, their eyes locked in a silent conversation, seemed determined to find closure on their own terms. But the armed figure, a wildcard in this twisted game, remained unmoved.

"There will be no closure," he snarled, his voice laced with a chilling finality. "There will only be retribution."

Just as he tightened his grip on the trigger, a deafening screech tore through the air. A set of headlights sliced through the darkness, illuminating the clearing like a stage set for a tragedy.

A police car skidded to a halt, two uniformed officers jumping out, their guns drawn. The unexpected arrival of the police, a beacon of authority in the chaos, caused the armed figure to hesitate.

He glanced at his gun, then at the officers with a mix of fear and defiance. Sensing his wavering resolve, Nadia seized the opportunity.

"Drop the weapon!" she shouted, her voice ringing out through the clearing.

The armed figure, startled by her sudden intervention, looked towards her. His eyes widened in recognition, a flicker of something akin to shame passing through them.

With a defeated sigh, he lowered the gun, its clatter echoing in the sudden silence. The officers rushed forward, securing the weapon and apprehending the suspect.

As the police led the handcuffed figure away, Nadia noticed a glimpse of a familiar red tie peeking out from under his jacket. A gasp escaped her lips – it was Ethan, the co-owner of the art gallery.

The revelation sent a fresh wave of confusion crashing down on her. What was Ethan's connection to Michael and Aisha? And why had he tried to take matters into his own hands?

Michael and Aisha, their faces etched with relief and exhaustion, turned towards each other. A silent understanding passed between them, a shared burden finally acknowledged.

David, his shoulders slumped in defeat, approached Nadia. "Nadia," he began, his voice hoarse with regret, "I—"

But Nadia held up a hand, silencing him. The words stuck in her throat, a bitter cocktail of anger and betrayal. The man she loved, the man she'd built a future with, was a stranger shrouded in a web of lies.

As the police took their statements, Nadia found herself drifting towards Aisha. The woman who had initially been a symbol of betrayal now appeared as a victim of circumstance, someone trapped in the shackles of the past.

Nine

Fractured Trust

The rising sun cast a faint glow on the clearing, painting the shattered remnants of the night's events in a harsh, unforgiving light. The police had finished their investigation, taking statements and securing evidence. Ethan, his defiance replaced by a sullen remorse, sat in the back of a police car, his head hanging low.

Nadia watched him go, a kaleidoscope of emotions swirling within her. The revelation that Ethan, the enigmatic art dealer, was somehow connected to Michael and Aisha, added another layer of complexity to the already tangled web of secrets.

David stood beside her, his presence a stark reminder of the deception he'd woven. "Nadia," he began, his voice thick with a plea for forgiveness.

She turned away from him, the sight of his face a painful reminder of the broken trust that lay between them. "Don't," she said, her voice barely a whisper.

"I owe you an explanation," he insisted, his voice tinged with desperation.

Nadia hesitated. A part of her craved the truth, the whole truth, but another part recoiled from the potential pain it might unleash. Finally, she turned back to him, her eyes filled with a mixture of anger and sadness.

"Tell me everything," she said, her voice firm despite the tremor running through her body. "Tell me about the accident, about Aisha, about Ethan."

David took a deep breath, his shoulders slumping under the weight of his past. He began to speak, his voice raspy from the night's ordeal. He recounted the story of his college romance with Aisha, their shared dreams and aspirations.

He spoke of the fateful night – a reckless drive on a rainy road, a sudden swerve to avoid a deer, and the sickening thud of metal on flesh. Aisha, he claimed, hadn't been behind the wheel as initially believed. She was the passenger, the one who bore the brunt of the crash.

David's guilt poured out of him, a torrent of regret for his silence and the life he'd built on a foundation of lies. He confessed his fear of losing Nadia, his cowardice in facing the past.

As David spoke, Nadia listened intently, each word etching itself onto her memory. The anger simmered within her, but it was tempered with a flicker of understanding. David's pain, though masked by deception, was real.

When he finished, a heavy silence descended upon them. The weight of his confession hung heavy in the air, a tangible manifestation of the shattered trust between them.

"Nadia," David said, his voice trembling, "I know I don't deserve it, but can you ever forgive me?"

Nadia didn't have an answer. Forgiveness felt like a distant hope, a bridge that would need to be rebuilt, brick by painstaking brick. The love she thought they shared now felt tainted, the foundation eroded by David's lies.

Her gaze fell on Aisha, who stood a few feet away, her face turned towards the rising sun. The woman who had been a symbol of betrayal now looked like a ghost from the past, finally released from the prison of her guilt.

Nadia took a tentative step towards Aisha, drawn by a strange sense of empathy. "Are you alright?" she asked softly.

Aisha turned, a flicker of surprise crossing her face before it settled into a melancholic smile. "I'm alive," she replied, her voice a mere whisper. "That's all that matters."

The simple statement resonated deeply with Nadia. Life, even a life marred by tragedy, was precious. David's betrayal had forced her to confront a harsh truth, but it had also shown her a different side of the love story she thought she knew.

As the sun climbed higher in the sky, casting its warm light on the clearing, Nadia knew she was at a crossroads. Her relationship with David hung in the balance, a fragile thing fractured by his deceit.

Could she rebuild trust? Could she forgive him? Or was their love story, like the shattered vase in the gallery, beyond repair? Only time, and the strength of the love that remained, would tell.

Ten

Whispers in the Wind

Days bled into weeks, a heavy silence settling over Nadia's apartment. David had left, taking with him a suitcase full of clothes and a heart brimming with regret. No calls, no texts, just the deafening silence that echoed the void left by his betrayal.

Nadia found solace in routine. Work at the library offered a welcome escape, the familiar scent of old paper and the hushed whispers of turning pages a balm to her troubled soul. Yet, amidst the stacks of books, the ghost of David lingered – his lingering gaze across the breakfast table, the warmth of his touch, the echo of his laughter in forgotten corners of their shared life.

One afternoon, a familiar face appeared at the library entrance. Amelia, her eyes filled with concern, approached Nadia's desk.

"Nadia," she began, her voice gentle, "how are you holding up?"

Nadia managed a weak smile. "It's…complicated," she admitted, her voice thick with unshed tears.

Amelia nodded, her gaze understanding. The news of David's deception, the revelation of Aisha and the chilling scene at the Whispering Palms, had spread like wildfire through their social circle.

"There's something you might want to see," Amelia said, her voice hushed. "Something that might shed some light on all this."

Intrigued, Nadia followed Amelia to a secluded corner of the library. Amelia retrieved a worn file from a dusty archive, its edges frayed and its pages brittle with age.

"This," Amelia explained, carefully placing the file on the table, "is Ethan's family history."

Nadia's brow furrowed. What could Ethan, the unassuming art dealer, have to do with her situation?

Amelia opened the file, revealing faded photographs and handwritten documents. As Nadia delved deeper, a gasp escaped her lips. The photographs depicted a young Ethan, his youthful smile mirroring the one in the picture of Aisha she'd found in the locket.

The documents confirmed it – Ethan was Aisha's younger brother. His presence at the Whispering Palms, his anger directed at David, suddenly made sense.

The file also contained a newspaper clipping, its yellowed edges whispering of a bygone era. The headline screamed: "Local Artist Killed in Tragic Accident." The accompanying photograph bore an uncanny resemblance to the accident Nadia had heard described.

The picture, however, wasn't of Aisha. It was of a young woman with vibrant eyes and a smile that held a striking familiarity – Amelia.

A wave of shock washed over Nadia. The pieces of the puzzle were finally falling into place, but the picture they revealed was far more complex than she could have ever imagined.

"Amelia," Nadia stammered, her voice trembling, "that's… that's you in the picture."

Amelia nodded, a tear rolling down her cheek. "Yes," she whispered, her voice raw with emotion. "The accident… it took my sister from me."

Suddenly, the fragmented stories – David's guilt, Aisha's grief, Ethan's rage – converged in Nadia's mind, forming a tragic narrative. Amelia's sister, not Aisha, had been the passenger in the car the night of the accident.

But then, who was Aisha, and what was her connection to David?

As Nadia voiced her confusion, Amelia took a deep breath. "There's more," she confessed. "The truth, the whole truth, has been buried for far too long."

She explained how Amelia, devastated by her sister's death and consumed by grief, had blamed David for the accident. She couldn't bear the thought of him moving on, finding happiness with another woman.

Desperate to keep David from ever experiencing a love that could be so brutally ripped away, Amelia had orchestrated a cruel deception. She'd convinced Aisha, with whom she'd shared a strained relationship due to their sibling rivalry, to pose as the passenger in the accident.

Aisha, burdened by a lifetime of guilt over a rift with Amelia, had agreed. It was a desperate act of reconciliation, a twisted attempt to mend a broken bond.

The revelation left Nadia breathless. Amelia, driven by grief and a warped sense of justice, had entangled everyone in a web of lies. It was a tragic chain reaction, a single act of deception that had poisoned lives for years.

"But why now?" Nadia questioned, her voice heavy. "Why after all these years?"

Amelia wiped away a stray tear. "Seeing you with David," she admitted, "seeing you happy… it awakened something within me. The guilt, the regret, it became too much to bear."

The realization stung. Her love for David, a relationship built on a foundation of deceit, had inadvertently triggered a chain of confessions, forcing Amelia to confront the painful truth of her actions.

The silence in the library stretched, thick with the weight of

Eleven

Unfinished Symphony

The library, once a refuge, now felt like a tomb of unearthed secrets. Nadia stared at Amelia, the woman she thought she knew, the woman whose kindness had always been a beacon. Now, Amelia stood shrouded in the shadows of her past, a ghost of the person Nadia had admired.

"I don't know what to say," Nadia finally admitted, her voice barely a whisper. The revelations had shattered her world, leaving her adrift in a sea of uncertainty.

A flicker of pain crossed Amelia's face. "I understand," she said, her voice hoarse. "There are no excuses for what I've done. I took away your happiness, your chance at a genuine love."

Shame bloomed in Amelia's eyes, a stark contrast to the defiance Nadia had expected. The woman before her wasn't a villain, but a broken soul consumed by remorse.

"But why Aisha?" Nadia asked, her voice laced with a newfound empathy. "Why drag her into this?"

Amelia sighed, the weight of the years etched on her face. "My grief was blinding," she confessed. "I couldn't bear the thought of David finding happiness again. Aisha... she was vulnerable, burdened by her own guilt. I convinced her it would be a way to make amends, to honor my sister."

The truth, even twisted as it was, painted a tragic picture. Amelia, crippled by her loss, had weaponized grief, wielding it like a cruel blade against David and unwittingly harming Aisha as well.

Nadia's gaze drifted to the faded photograph of Aisha clutched tightly in her hand. The woman in the picture, once a symbol of betrayal, now seemed like a pawn in a twisted game orchestrated by Amelia's despair.

A fresh wave of questions bombarded Nadia. Where was Aisha now? And how badly had she been affected by the years spent carrying the weight of a lie?

"Do you know where Aisha is?" Nadia asked, her voice filled with a desperate urgency.

Amelia shook her head, sadness clouding her eyes. "The last I heard, she moved away shortly after the accident. Unable to bear the memories, she started anew."

Nadia's heart ached for Aisha, a woman who had been a victim twice over – first in the accident, then in Amelia's elaborate charade. Their lives, seemingly unconnected, had been tragically intertwined by a single, devastating event.

"What about David?" Nadia asked, a knot forming in her stomach. "Did he know about this?"

Amelia's silence spoke volumes. The pain etched on her face confirmed Nadia's deepest fear – David had been kept in the dark, manipulated by Amelia's deception.

Fury bubbled within Nadia. How could David not have questioned the lack of a police report, the absence of Aisha from his life for so long? Yet, a part of her understood – love, sometimes, could blind one to the truth.

The revelation of Amelia's role changed everything. David's silence, previously interpreted as deceit, now seemed more like a desperate attempt to hold onto the happiness he'd built with Nadia, a happiness he'd unknowingly stolen from someone else.

A storm of emotions – anger, betrayal, but also a flicker of a strange understanding – warred within Nadia. The path forward seemed treacherous, a tangled web of lies and broken trust.

But amidst the chaos, a single thought remained clear - the truth, however painful, had finally surfaced. It was a starting point, a foundation upon which a new future could be built, if it was even possible.

Nadia rose from her chair, her mind buzzing with unanswered questions. "I need time," she said, her voice firm despite the turmoil within. "Time to process everything, to figure out where to go from here."

Amelia nodded, understanding etched on her face. "I understand," she said, her voice barely above a whisper. "And Nadia, I'm truly sorry. For all the pain I've caused."

Nadia offered a weak smile, a gesture more for Amelia's sake than her own. The weight of forgiveness felt daunting, but the desire to somehow mend the broken pieces of their lives flickered tentatively within her.

Stepping out of the library, Nadia was greeted by the bustling city street. The once familiar sights and sounds now seemed muted, colored by the stark reality she had just unearthed.

She needed answers, not just about David and Aisha, but about her own desires and what she truly wanted from the future that lay ahead. The melody of their love story, once vibrant and full of promise, now played out in a disjointed, discordant rhythm.

Could the symphony be restarted? Could they rewrite the score, or were the notes of their love forever tainted by the painful chords of the past? The path forward was uncertain, a question mark hanging heavy in the air. Nadia took a deep

Twelve

Echoes of the Past

Chap

Months had bled into one another, seasons shifting like the ever-changing emotions within Nadia's heart. The revelations at the Whispering Palms had left an indelible mark, a constant reminder of the intricate web of lies that had ensnared her life.

David had reached out, his words filled with remorse and a desperate hope for reconciliation. Nadia, however, had retreated into a shell of self-protection, her mind a battleground between anger and a lingering love.

One breezy afternoon, while sorting through a box of old clothes, Nadia stumbled upon a familiar worn leather satchel tucked away in a forgotten corner. It was David's. Curiosity piqued, she unlatched the forgotten bag, its contents releasing a wave of memories.

Sketches adorned with familiar landscapes, remnants of their shared travels, tumbled out. A half-written poem, its words echoing their whispered promises, lay nestled amongst crumpled receipts and forgotten trinkets.

As she sifted through the mementos, a worn postcard slipped from a hidden compartment. The picture on the front depicted a quaint seaside town bathed in the golden glow of the setting sun. On the back, a scribbled message sent a jolt through Nadia:

"Aisha. Finally found peace. Hope you can too. Come visit sometime. Love, David."

The blood drained from Nadia's face. David had found Aisha. A cocktail of emotions – relief, anger, and a pang of jealousy – warred within her.

Suddenly, the need to know, to understand, became an unyielding urge. She grabbed her phone, her finger hovering over David's number before dialing a different one – Amelia's.

A few days later, Amelia stood on Nadia's doorstep, her gaze filled with apprehension. Without a word, Nadia thrust the postcard into Amelia's hand.

Amelia's eyes widened as she recognized the picture and David's handwriting. Shame flushed her cheeks as she read the message.

"He found her," Amelia finally said, her voice barely a whisper.

Nadia nodded, a question hanging in the air. Amelia took a deep breath. "They reconnected a few months ago," she explained. "David felt the need to apologize, to finally come clean about everything."

"And Aisha?" Nadia asked, her voice trembling slightly.

"She forgave him," Amelia said, a flicker of surprise crossing her face. "She understood his pain, his silence all these years."

Nadia's heart clenched. It seemed forgiveness, however elusive, was possible. But what about her? Could she ever forgive David for the lie that had colored their entire relationship?

Sensing Nadia's turmoil, Amelia reached out and placed a hand on her arm. "Nadia," she said, her voice gentle, "you deserve happiness. Whatever decision you make, make it for yourself, for the life you want to live."

The words struck a chord deep within Nadia. The burden of choice, once a paralyzing weight, now felt oddly liberating.

Over the next few weeks, Nadia wrestled with her emotions. Anger ebbed, replaced by a quiet understanding of the complexities of the past. The love she felt for David, though tainted, still flickered within her.

One day, a handwritten note arrived in the mail. The familiar, slightly crooked script sent a shiver down Nadia's spine. It wasn't from David, but from Aisha.

The note was brief, filled with gratitude for Nadia's understanding and a heartfelt invitation to visit the seaside town pictured on the postcard. It was a simple gesture, an olive branch extended across the chasm of time and deceit.

Holding the note, Nadia finally understood. Forgiveness wasn't about erasing the past, but about acknowledging the hurt and finding a way to move forward.

She didn't know if her future lay with David, but she knew that she could finally face it with a heart unburdened by the weight of secrets.

With a deep breath, Nadia packed a bag, a single postcard tucked safely inside. The journey ahead, like the melody of a half-finished symphony, remained uncertain. But this time, Nadia held the pen, ready to write a new chapter, a chapter filled with the echoes of the past, but also with the promise of a future yet to be defined.

Milton Keynes UK
Ingram Content Group UK Ltd.
UKHW022159040824
446478UK00001B/81